Holiday Hidden Treasures

Hidden Picture Puzzles
for
Special Celebrations
by
Liz Ball

HOW MANY

PARTY TIME

FUN

I FOUND SOME!

MORE THAN 1200 HIDDEN OBJECTS!

WHAT IS YOUR FAVORITE DAY?

56 Pages of Fun

With love to Bob, Trent and Alicia

HAVE FUN!!

Celebrate

Copyright 2000 by Liz Ball
As featured in the Dayton Daily News
All rights reserved
2nd Edition

Published by Hidden Pictures
P.O. Box 63
Tipp City, OH 45371
Printed in the USA
www.Hidden-Pictures.com

MW01091766

HAVE A "BEARY" HAPPY VALENTINE'S DAY!

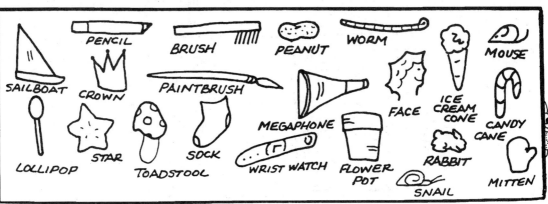

PENCIL   BRUSH   PEANUT   WORM   MOUSE

SAILBOAT   CROWN   PAINTBRUSH   MEGAPHONE   FACE   ICE CREAM CONE   CANDY CANE

LOLLIPOP   STAR   TOADSTOOL   SOCK   WRIST WATCH   FLOWER POT   RABBIT   MITTEN

SNAIL

CUPCAKE LADLE TROWEL (2) SAILBOAT EASTER EGG ARTIST BRUSH MITTEN (2) BATS POPSICLE (2) HEARTS NEEDLE

(2) TEPEES EYE GLASSES BUTTERFLIES (2) FIREFLY

(2) SOCKS SNAKE CANOE RAT CROWN SALT SHAKER

RAINBOW DREAMS

Jelly Bean Lane →

HAPPY EASTER

RING
CARROT
SOCK
SHOE
CROWN
(2) FISH
PENCIL
TEPEE
ACORN
CROSS
(2) BRUSHES
TOAST
(2) BIRDS
FOOT-BALL
AXE
CONE
CANDLE
UMBRELLA
IRON
BUTTERFLY
ORCA
SPOON

Liz Ball

ALLIGATOR

NEEDLE

MOON

CROSS

PEAR

LADDER

PITCHER

PAINT BRUSH

CAMEL

HAMMER

TURTLE

HOUSE

TEPEE

BIRD

SNAKE

ICE CREAM CONE

FISH HOOK

BANANA

BOWL

CROWN

CUP

HAPPY EASTER

blue

PINK

Yellow

GRADUATION

Hooray!

NEEDLE
HOUSE
DUCK
CARROT
ALLIGATOR
SPIDER
RING
FISH
PENCIL
BUTTERFLY
SALTSHAKER
FROG
PENGUIN
SNAKE
SPOON
ZEBRA
SHOE
CROWN
HEART
BEETLE

MEMORIAL DAY

CUP DOG HEAD (2) SPOONS BATON
(3) SOCKS STING RAY ART BRUSH
PENCIL CARROT CRAYFISH
SAILBOAT BIRD
RULER (3) CONES LADDER ARROWHEAD FLOWER POT VIAL
BIKINI BRA HEART

©Liz Ball

MEMORIAL DAY

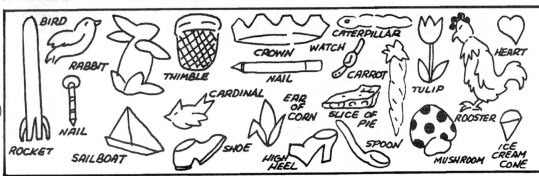

BIRD

RABBIT

THIMBLE

CROWN

WATCH

CATERPILLAR

TULIP

HEART

NAIL

CARROT

CARDINAL

EAR OF CORN

SLICE OF PIE

ROOSTER

ROCKET

NAIL

SAILBOAT

SHOE

HIGH HEEL

SPOON

MUSHROOM

ICE CREAM CONE

RICE

E.C.
+
R.B.

(4) CARROTS   RING   GOBLET

(2) BIRDS   TEPEE   OWL   DIAMOND

SOCK   CUPCAKE

TOP HAT   CONE

SALT SHAKER   ART BRUSH   BELL

CANDLE   SLICE of CAKE   CAKE SERVER   WATCH

LOVEBIRDS

GARTER

CAKE KNIFE   (3) DOVES

CROSS   OLD SHOE

WEDDING
CAKE   DIAMOND   (3) HEARTS   SOCK   (2) CANDLES   (2) MUSIC NOTES   CHAMPAGNE GLASSES (2)

WEDDING
RING

(2) BELLS

My dad's name is Merle. What is your dad's name?

HAPPY FATHER'S DAY

DAD

My dad is SUPER!

EcBall

COOKING PAN

CUP

NEEDLE

ELF SHOE

SNAKE

RABBIT

SODA

IRON

CARROT

LOAF OF BREAD

LADDER

(3) BIRDS

BOAT

POT

TOOTHBRUSH

TURTLE

BUTTERFLY

BOWLING PIN

APPLE CORE

KNIFE

CONE

MOUSE

NATIVE AMERICANS DAY

CROWN SLICE OF ORANGE TURTLE SPOON FLASHLIGHT BIRD

CAMEL TENNIS BALL HARE CONE SAILBOAT COMB LOLLIPOP CUP BRUSH AXE ARTIST BRUSH

WORM

ARROWHEAD
COMB
CUP
HOTDOG
SPOON
BANANA
OLD FASHION KEY
BOW
HOUSE
TEPEE
CANOE
UMBRELLA
ARROW
WORM
HARE
(3) PENCILS
SOCK
MUSHROOM
STONE AXE HEAD
HAT
FLOWER POT

HAPPY GRANDPARENTS DAY

Hi Grandma

GRANDMA

HAPPY GRANDPARENTS DAY!

GRANDPA BUG

AXE

NEEDLE

HALO

SOCK

MOTH

CUPCAKE

ENVELOPE

CROWN

(2) SAILBOATS

TOOTHBRUSH

NECK-TIE

MEGAPHONE

CHERRY

RING

BOOMERANG

MATCH

MUSIC NOTES (2)

EARTHWORM

SPIDER

TABLE KNIFE

CROQUET BALL

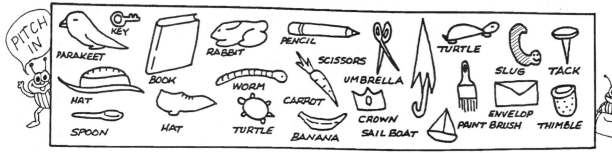

SHOE

(2) SOCKS

PIECE OF CANDY

BIRD

WISHBONE

TOOTHBRUSH

CONE

(14) HEARTS

PARTY HAT

SPOON

HORSE HEAD

WHEAT

LIGHTBULB

(3)
SHOES

PENCIL

MEGAPHONE

SAILBOAT

NEEDLE

FUNNEL

BRUSH

CATERPILLAR

IRON

SOCK

(2)
TEPEES

SPOON

WORM

PEN

CANDLESTICK HOLDER

WITCH'S HAT

THUMB TACK

BALLOON

KNIFE

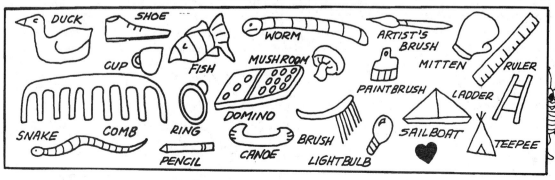

HAPPY
KWANZAA

RABBIT POCKET KNIFE BIRD SAILBOAT HEART FISH HOOK ICE CREAM CONE ENVELOP COMB CRAYON GLASSES DUCK

SHOE PENCIL TOOTHBRUSH WORM CUPCAKE (2) BOOKS LADDER CROWN PAINT BRUSH

SANTA'S WORKSHOP

PEACE ON EARTH

CANOE · STAR · HOLLY · PAN · BASEBALL · TEA CUP · SAILBOAT · PINE TREE · CROSS · SAILBOAT · ROCKET · PIE SLICE · GOLD RING · ICE CREAM CONE · BOWL · CARDINAL · RULER · WATCH · DONUT · HEART · CAKE SLICE · (4) STOCKINGS